One-Minute Stories of Brothers and Sisters

One-Minute Stories of Brothers and Sisters

Adapted by
Shari Lewis

Illustrated by
Kelly Oechsli

Doubleday
NEW YORK

Library of Congress Cataloging-in-Publication Data

Lewis, Shari.
    One-minute stories of brothers and sisters.

    Summary: A collection of twenty folk and fairy tales
about brothers and sisters all in a format for reading in
one minute.
    1. Fairy tales. 2. Tales. [1. Fairy tales. 2. Folklore.
3. Brothers and sisters—Folklore] I. Oechsli, Kelly, ill.
II. Title.
PZ8.L481250o   1988   398.2'7   [E]   87-20056
ISBN 0-385-23425-2

CONTENTS

To the Parents

As a child, I always wondered why my folks were so eager for my sister and me to be friends. Now that I'm a grown-up, I think I know: Parents realize that they won't be around forever, and they hope their children will provide lifelong support systems for one another.

So parents endlessly repeat, "In your brother [or sister], you have someone you'll always be able to count on."

But kids tend to be ornery, and parents pushing the value of one sibling to another, as mine did, are likely to create an opposite, undesired effect. You can't legislate love and companionship merely by insisting, "You two should be friends!"

Kids learn best by indirection—and there's no more painless way to make a point than through a story. Good stories provide role models for loving relationships (read about the big billy goats Gruff brother who butted in when his little brother was threatened, or Svetlana, who went all the way up to the

Sun to help her brother, Davit. And, in a British tale, Ann wouldn't desert her sister Kate, even though she had been turned into a sheep!).

Jean Houston (author of *Searching for the Beloved)* says, "Stories play upon your mind like an instrument." These *One-Minute Stories of Brothers and Sisters* sing a song of sibling success—the hero or heroine is yanked from the fire by the superhuman efforts of a sister or brother who just won't give up, in spite of the odds. And the message is clear: if you and your sibling are pulling together, one plus one will always equal much more than two.

Shari Lewis

Tiki Tiki Timbo

Chinese

Here's the story of a Chinese boy whose name was . . .
     Ti Ki Ti Ki Timbo No Sin Nimbo
     Hoi Doi Bos Ki Poi Pon Do Hi Ki
     Pon Pon Ni Ki, No Mi Ah Dom Poi

In those days in China, if you really loved your child, the way to show it was to give your child a long name. The longer, the better. Now this little boy—
     Ti Ki Ti Ki Timbo No Sin Nimbo
     Hoi Doi Bos Ki Poi Pon Do Hi Ki,
     Pon Pon Ni Ki, No Mi Ah Dom Poi

had a brother whose name was Choy. Obviously, Choy was not the favorite, but the brothers *were* friends.

8

One day, picking apples on a tree whose branches reached over a well,

> Ti Ki Ti Ki Timbo No Sin Nimbo
> Hoi Doi Bos Ki Poi Pon Do Hi Ki,
> Pon Pon Ni Ki, No Mi Ah Dom Poi

fell to the bottom of the well.

Choy ran home and gasped, "Mama, your other son,

> Ti Ki Ti Ki Timbo No Sin Nimbo
> Hoi Doi Bos Ki Poi Pon Do Hi Ki,
> Pon Pon Ni Ki, No Mi Ah Dom Poi

has fallen to the bottom of the well."

Well, that took so long to say that by the time they got the ladder and reached Ti Ki Ti Ki—oh, you know who I mean—he had almost drowned.

And that may be why today, very few of us are given names quite as long as that!

9

Maya-Mayi

Australian

Lonely Wurrunna set out to look for a wife. He came to a camp belonging to seven young girls. "We are the Maya-mayi sisters," they told him, "and we're only visiting this country." The sisters invited Wurrunna to share their campfire.

Next morning, Wurrunna left, pretending to continue his journey, but his plan was to capture a couple of the sisters and take them as wives. He hid in the bushes until he saw his chance, then grabbed two of the girls and ran away with them.

After a while, Wurrunna stopped for lunch. "Strip some bark from those two trees," he ordered, "so I can build a fire."

"We will never come back," said the sisters.

"If you try to run away, I'll catch you," said Wurrunna.

So each sister swung her stone ax into a tree. The axes stuck fast, and two trees began to grow. They quickly rose higher and higher with the sisters clinging to their axes until the trees had reached heaven.

Then the other five sisters appeared in the sky and helped the two in the trees to climb up and join them amidst the clouds. Those seven sisters turned into stars in the night sky, which are called the Mayamayi by the Australian aborigines.

And as for lonely Wurrunna, why, he's *still* looking for a wife.

Kate and Ann

English

Ann's sister Kate was so beautiful, no one looked at Ann when Kate was in the room. But Ann didn't mind because she loved Kate very much. However, the queen *was* jealous, and paid a witch to change pretty Kate into a sheep. Ann, horrified to see the sheep dressed in her sister's clothes, grabbed Kate by her collar and ran away from the palace.

Late that night, Ann led Kate to *another* palace and asked for food and a place to sleep. "Only if you'll sit up with the sick prince, who cannot be cured," said the king who lived there. Ann agreed, and she and

12

her sheepish sister were taken to the prince. When they were alone, the prince tiptoed downstairs to his horse. Ann followed him. He rode into the woods with Ann just behind and entered a cave in a hillside.

In the cavern, the fairy princesses were having a ball. The prince danced the night away with one fairy princess after another, and then rode back home to his room.

At the ball, Ann had picked up a magic wand dropped by one of the fairies. Now, she touched her sister Kate with it. Instantly Kate was transformed from a sheep back into her beautiful self. Next, Ann touched the sick prince with the wand and made him well, too. The king was so pleased, he gave Ann the prince for her husband, and the prince's brother married Kate, in spite of the fact that she still occasionally grazed on the front lawn!

Rama and His Half Brother

East Indian

King Dasaratha loved his first wife best, for she was mother of Prince Rama. When she died, the king's second wife had a son named Bharata.

"Someday *my* son, Bharata, shall be king," said the new queen.

"No, Rama is the elder," said Dasaratha. *"He* will inherit the throne."

But the king didn't trust the new queen, and said to Prince Rama, "Hide in the woods. In twelve years, I'll be dead. Then come back and be king."

But the king died after only nine years. The queen tried to make her son Bharata put on the crown, but he said, "No, only my older half brother, Rama, can be king." Bharata found Rama in the woods.

"Time for you to become king, my brother," Bharata said to Rama. But Rama explained that he was supposed to return after *twelve* years, not nine. "Take my slippers back with you and let them rule in my place."

So for three years, Rama's slippers ran the country, hopping up and down on the throne when they were displeased with anything. Then Rama took over and was king for sixteen thousand years, which is a long time, even in India.

The Golden Lads

German

A fisherman caught a golden fish which said, "Cut me into four pieces. Feed two pieces to your wife, and plant the other two in the garden." Nobody argues with a golden, talking fish, so the fisherman did as he was told.

The two pieces of fish planted in the garden grew into a pair of golden lilies, and the wife gave birth to two golden baby boys. When the brothers were grown, one married a maiden in a distant village.

One morning, hunting deep in the woods, the married brother stopped to rest near a witch's hut. The witch's little dog ran to the golden lad, barking and snapping at his ankles. The boy shouted, "Get away, mutt, or I'll—" "You'll do nothing of the sort!" screamed the witch from a window of her hut, and she turned the golden brother to stone.

Meanwhile, back at the fisherman's place, the other brother noticed that one of the golden lilies was stretched out dead on the ground. "My brother's in trouble!" he shouted, and he galloped to the witch's hut. He pointed his bow and arrow at the witch until she made the stone brother as alive and golden as ever.

At home, the golden lily that had seemed dead now stood up and put out a golden bloom, and once again the two golden brothers went their separate ways, to live long and happy lives.

Svetlana and Davit
Russian

Svetlana's brother Davit was a hunter. One day, Davit became so sick he couldn't get out of bed. Svetlana went up to the heavens to beg the Sun for help.

An old woman was standing on the clouds. Svetlana asked, "How can I meet the Sun?"

"I'm his mother," said the woman. "Can I help?"

Svetlana told her about Davit's illness, and the old woman said, "My son, the Sun, doesn't like humans much, so I'd better turn you into a broom and stand you in the corner. When my son, the Sun, comes home, I'll find out what I can."

When the Sun came home, his mother remarked, "Well, son, have the humans been behaving themselves?"

"All but a hunter named Davit," answered the Sun. "He made so much noise with his gun, it got on my nerves. I had to cast a spell on him to keep him quiet. But don't be upset, Mother—if he'll stay in a dark room for seventeen days, he'll be good as new."

As soon as the Sun had gone to bed, his mother changed Svetlana from a broom back into herself, and the girl returned to earth. She kept Davit in a dark room for seventeen days and, sure enough, he got well. And to make sure the Sun didn't become angry again, Svetlana took away Davit's gun. He found a quieter line of work, and was healthy for the rest of his days.

The Three Billy Goats Gruff
Norwegian

Three billy goats named Gruff wanted to graze in a meadow across the river, but the bridge was guarded by a mean troll.

The smallest goat tried to cross first and the troll yelled, "Who dares cross my bridge? It must be my supper!" Frightened, the little goat told the troll, "I'll scarcely make a nibble for you. Let me pass. A fatter goat is coming. The troll thought (as much as trolls can think) and then said, "Go on. I will eat *you* on your way home."

The medium-sized goat started to cross and the same meanie said, "Who dares cross my bridge? It must be my supper!" The goat said, "The goat behind me can feed you for a month. Eat me, and you'll be too tired to catch *him.*" The troll let this goat pass, too.

Finally, the biggest billy goat Gruff started across the bridge and *was* big, with huge horns and hooves. The troll

called, "Who dares cross my bridge?" But before he could fin-
ish, the big goat rammed him with his horns and stomped him
with his hooves and kicked the troll into the deep river where
he was never heard from again.

Of course, why that *biggest* goat didn't just cross the
bridge first is a mystery to me!

23

The Lazy Brothers

Majorcan

In his will, a dying father asked the judge to give the father's donkey to whichever of his three sons was the laziest.

At the courthouse, the judge said, "You'll have to convince me which of you is lazier than the others." The boys yawned, and the eldest one said, "I am so lazy that one day, a red hot ember flew in my lap and I would have gone up in flames if my father hadn't thrown a bucket of water on me."

"Well," said the second brother, "I'm so lazy that when I fell into the ocean, the thought of trying to save myself ex-

hausted me, and I would have drowned if some sailors hadn't pulled me out."

The judge said, "What about you?" to the third brother who was lying face down on the floor. The boy sighed deeply and said, "Oh, your honor, put me in jail. I'd rather lose the donkey than wear myself out talking.."

Of course, the judge gave the donkey to the last boy and ordered all the three lazy brothers thrown out of the courthouse onto the street where they remained for three years, too lazy even to go home.

The Wonderful Hammer
Japanese

Kira, a poor man, was kind and generous. His rich brother, Cho, was greedy and jealous.

One day, a flock of birds was eating the green sprouts in Kira's rice paddy. He chased them away, then lay down for a nap and dreamed of children playing with a magic hammer. When he woke up, the hammer was lying beside him.

And sure enough, that hammer granted all Kira's wishes, which soon made him richer than his brother Cho.

When Cho learned of the magic hammer, he insisted that Kira tell him how he'd gotten it. Then Cho rushed to his own rice paddy, waited for a flock of birds, chased them and lay down for a nap. Children appeared in *his* dream, too, but instead of playing, they made fun of Cho for being greedy, and pulled hard on his nose until it hung down to his chest like an elephant's. When he awoke, he had this ridiculous nose, but no magic hammer. He ran to his brother Kira, who said, "I'll help you if you promise not to be greedy and jealous anymore." Cho truly promised. Kira wished upon his magic hammer that Cho's nose would shrink, and then Kira tapped Cho on the nose with it. At that, Cho's nose became less generous, just as his heart became more so.

One-Eye, Two-Eyes, and Three-Eyes

German

One-Eye and Three-Eyes were mean to their sister Two-Eyes. Why? Because she only had two eyes, and she looked so ordinary. Every day, they sent her away to look after the goat without even giving her breakfast.

Her fairy godmother said, "Poor Two-Eyes. If you're hungry, just say, 'Little Goat, come here. Little Table, appear.' " Two-Eyes did, and there was a table covered with food. She ate her fill, told the table to vanish, and went home content.

But now the mean sisters became suspicious, because Two-Eyes stopped complaining. So One-Eye went along to mind the goat, to see if she could discover Two-Eyes' secret. But Two-Eyes put her sister One-Eye's one eye to sleep with a lullaby. Then she said,

"Little Goat, come here. Little Table, appear!" and enjoyed her lunch.

Next day, Three-Eyes went along. Two-Eyes sang, but the lullaby only put two of Three-Eyes' eyes to sleep, and the third eye saw everything. The mean sister killed the goat, which made Two-Eyes weep. But her fairy godmother said, "Don't cry, silly. Bury the goat's heart and see what happens."

Two-Eyes did, and the following morning, a golden tree covered with golden fruit had grown in that very spot! The fruit only came off the tree for *her*, so Two-Eyes was never hungry again.

Ricardo, Roberto, Alfredo, and Bernardo

Spanish

The four Ramirez brothers left home and went their separate ways. When they met a year later, Ricardo had become a swimming champion, Roberto an expert with a gun, and Alfredo had gotten hold of a pair of glasses that enabled him to see great distances. But nothing adventuresome had happened to Bernardo. He had only become a carpenter and woodcutter.

Together again, the brothers set out in a boat to rescue a princess who was the prisoner of a giant sea serpent. From the boat, Alfredo could see through his glasses that the monster was asleep, so the swimming champion, Ricardo, swam ashore and rescued the princess. But as they escaped, their splashing awakened the serpent, and it followed them back to the boat, fire spewing from its nose. Taking aim with his rifle, Roberto shot the serpent, but with one final last lash of its tail, the creature cut the wooden boat in two, and they thought they'd drown. "Don't worry," said Bernardo, "carpentry is my craft." He pulled out his tools and made the boat as good as new.

Of all the brothers, the king chose Bernardo to marry the princess because without his ability to fix things, his daughter would have been lost. He said, "Heroes are fine for high adventure, but woodworkers make handy husbands."

The Forest Bride

Finnish

Three brothers decided to look for wives. "Each of us shall cut down a tree and go in the direction in which it falls." They agreed.

The older brother's tree fell toward farmland, and the second brother's toward a village. But the youngest brother's tree pointed at the deep forest where nobody lived. In no time, the first two found nice brides, but the youngest brother had no luck in the woods. The only living creature he came upon was a little mouse. "Only a mouse!" he groaned. "I need a sweetheart."

"I'll be your sweetheart," said the mouse. The boy laughed at the idea, but the longer he stayed, the more he liked her, and finally he decided to take her home.

The mouse hopped into a walnut-shell carriage drawn by five other mice, and away they went. But a stranger, running on the path, accidentally stepped on the little carriage and crushed it, mouse and all.

The boy sat down and cried. "Sweetheart?" said a soft voice. "Won't you come sit by me?" When the boy looked up, he saw that the walnut-shell carriage had turned into a golden coach, the little mice into five black horses, and in the coach sat a lovely princess. "You liked me when I was only a mouse," she said. "Now that the spell is broken, can't you still like me?"

"I can sure try!" said he. That's how the youngest brother came to marry the princess, and now the other two brothers visit their youngest brother at the palace as often as they can.

The Well of the Moon
Majorcan

A witch turned three princesses into stones and threw them into a dry well. Their father, the king, offered a reward to anyone who could find the sisters and save them. Many tried but failed. However, a poor peasant boy named Bernard had the good sense to be kind to an old beggar who turned out to be a sorcerer.

"In a bottle, collect water from seven magic wells," said the sorcerer. "Next, lower yourself to the bottom of the Well of the Moon."

There, Bernard found the three stones that had once been princesses. These stones were guarded by a serpent, a lion,

and a devil with a forked tail. As the old beggar had instructed him, Bernie threw the magic water from his bottle onto the beasts, and the serpent and the lion both disappeared.

But the devil wrestled the boy to the ground. Fighting for his life, Bernard bit off the devil's right ear, which, amazingly enough, was *just* what you had to do to destroy his evil powers.

"I'll give you your ear only if you'll turn these stones back into princesses," said Bernard, and the devil agreed.

At that, everybody went away happy except the devil, who put his ear on backward, and from that day to this keeps losing his glasses.

The Fools Who Married Fools
Icelandic

Brenda complained to sister Ingrid that her husband, Ulrick, was a fool. Not to be outdone, Ingrid insisted that *her* husband, Wendel, was even *more* of a fool than Ulrick. The sisters decided to see which husband was more foolish.

That evening, when Ulrick came home he found Brenda busily sewing with needle and thread, but he couldn't see any cloth. Brenda claimed, "Oh, this cloth is too fine for you to see. Your eyesight isn't what it should be, but I'm sewing a suit of clothes for you that will make your friends envious." Ulrick couldn't *wait* to try on his new suit!

When Ingrid's husband Wendel came home from work, she scolded him for being on his feet, crying, "Have you forgotten that you died this morning? I've already ordered your coffin."

Next day, Wendel was carried to the cemetery in his coffin and Ulrick followed, proudly showing off his new suit. Of course, there *was* no new suit, so everyone laughed so to see Ulrick naked. The laughter caused Wendel to open his coffin to look. "Oh my," he said. "If I wasn't dead, I'd have to laugh, too!"

The sisters agreed that their husbands were equally foolish, but then, so were *they*, for marrying them!

Hansel and Gretel

German

Hansel and Gretel's mean stepmother wanted to get rid of them. She led them in circles in the woods until she thought they were lost and then left them there, asleep on the ground. When the children awoke, they weren't worried, for they had dropped a trail of bread crumbs to follow back to their house. But the sister and brother were horrified to find that birds had eaten the crumbs, so they really *were* lost!

Hansel and Gretel wandered through the woods until they came to a cabin built of cookies and candies and cake. Since they were hungry, they broke off bits of the roof and were happily stuffing themselves when who should appear but the witch who lived in the house.

She locked Hansel in a cage, saying, "I'm going to cook you for dinner!"

Then the witch told Gretel to crawl into the oven to see if it was hot. Gretel pretended not to know how, and tricked the witch into showing her. As soon as the witch poked her head into the oven, Gretel pushed the rest of her in as well, slammed the door, and set her brother free.

Then Hansel and Gretel ran home, told their father how mean the stepmother was, and he chased the stepmother away, which, as you can imagine, made these children as happy as children can be.

The Enchanted Brothers

Italian

Once upon a time, there were three brothers. For no reason at all, a wicked fairy turned one into a falcon (a big bird), the next into a stag (a male deer), and the third into a dolphin (a large friendly sea animal). Even so, each of the brothers married one of the king's three daughters, and they went to their separate palaces.

The falcon took his wife to a mountaintop, the stag carried her sister deep into the woods, and the last princess went with the dolphin to an island in the ocean.

They were visited by the girls' younger brother, Tittone. He was given a gift by each husband when he left. The falcon presented him with a special feather, the stag with a magic lock of hair, and the dolphin with an enchanted fish scale.

killed the dragon. And the dolphin made the waters of the lake rise until the tower disappeared forever!

Because this particular maiden was a very important princess, the wicked fairy's spell was broken, and the three enchanted brothers became nice young men once again, which probably helped their wives live happier lives.

On his way home, Tittone spotted a stone tower in a lake, guarded by a dragon. At the tower window stood a lovely maiden, just right for Tittone. Determined to rescue her, he wished upon his three gifts, and suddenly he was surrounded by his sisters' husbands.

The falcon called on his bird friends to fly the girl from the tower to safety. The stag brought together the wild animals of the forest and they

The Three Luck Children

German

Three poor brothers set out to sell what little they owned.

The first tried to peddle a rooster from town to town, but people all said, "Got all the roosters we need here!" Finally, on an island where there *were* no roosters, he announced, "Every morning, the cock will crow to let you know when the sun will rise. If he crows during the day, it means there will be a change in the weather." For that rooster, the island people gave the boy all the gold he could carry.

The second brother had a big curved knife. He found a country where people cut down their corn by shooting it with guns (which made a mess!). With his knife, the boy cut the whole corn crop without smashing a kernel. The country folk gave brother number two a wheelbarrowful of gold for his wonderful knife.

The third boy had a cat. As you can imagine, he had trouble finding a place where nobody had seen a cat, but luckily, when he did find such a place, it was overrun with mice. The cat caught their mice, and those people gratefully filled the third brother's pockets with gold.

Rumor has it that, by then, the three brothers were rich enough to build themselves a fine house and never travel anywhere for the rest of their lives.

Snow White and Rose Red

German

The twin sisters Snow White and Rose Red lived in a cottage in the woods. One winter, a big black bear knocked on their door and asked if he could come in out of the cold. The bear became a regular guest and a playmate for the sisters, but in spring he went away and didn't return.

One day, the sisters came across a little man with his beard caught in a tree. "Help me, you idiots!" screeched the dwarf. The girls pulled and tugged and finally had to cut the dwarf's beard loose with their scissors. He picked up a sack of gold and ran off without so much as a "thank you." The following after-

noon, in a clearing in the woods, Snow White and Rose Red stumbled upon the same dwarf counting a pile of gold nearly as big as he was. Suddenly their friend, the big black bear, stepped out of the woods and killed the dwarf with one mighty smack. The bear's skin fell away and there stood a wonderful prince. "That villain turned me into a bear," said the prince. "The only way I could break the spell was to kill him."

Rose Red married the prince, and Snow White married his brother, who showed up just in time to divide the dwarf's treasure, which apparently had belonged to the two brothers to begin with!

Little Brother

American Indian

Bear-Chief looked after all the bears in the forest from his cave in Bear Mountain.

In a nearby tepee lived the Indian boy, Little Brother, and his two big brothers. With their bows and arrows, the big brothers killed bears for food. Each time they killed a bear, its ghost complained to Bear-Chief.

So Bear-Chief tricked the big brothers into his cave and turned them into bear-boys, with fur on their arms and legs.

Little Brother left the tepee to save his big brothers. But the deep snow made it hard for Little Brother to walk fast. He begged his snowshoes for help, and they flew him through the air and set him down right in front of Bear Mountain.

46

"Bear-Chief!" shouted Little Brother. "Let my big brothers come out or I'll tear down your mountain." Bear-Chief laughed, so Little Brother shot an arrow into the mountain and cracked it open. His two big brothers came out on all fours like bears, but in the daylight the fur fell off their limbs, and once again they stood on their hind legs like normal Indian boys.

Bear-Chief had to find another place to live, and that's probably why there are barely any bears in the neighborhood these days.

About the Author

World-famous ventriloquist and puppeteer Shari Lewis (also known as Lamb Chop's mother) has been honored with five Emmy Awards, a Peabody, the Monte Carlo TV Award for World's Best Variety Show, and the 1983 Kennedy Center Award for Excellence and Creativity in the Arts. One of the few female symphony conductors, she has performed with and conducted more than one hundred symphony orchestras, including the National Symphony at the Kennedy Center, the Pittsburgh Symphony, the National Arts Centre Orchestra of Canada, and the Osaka National Symphony in Japan.

In addition to the recently published *One-Minute Christmas Stories*, Shari Lewis is the author of *One-Minute Bedtime Stories*, *One-Minute Favorite Fairy Tales*, *One-Minute Animal Stories*, *One-Minute Bible Stories—Old Testament*, *One-Minute Bible Stories—New Testament*, and *One-Minute Greek Myths*. A number of the *One-Minute* books are available on videocassettes, as well as audio cassettes.

Shari Lewis is presently chairman of the Board of Trustees of the International Reading Foundation and has served on the national board of the Girl Scouts of the U.S.A. A resident of Beverly Hills, California, Ms. Lewis is married to book publisher Jeremy Tarcher; their daughter, Mallory, is in the home video industry.

About the Illustrator

Kelly Oechsli has illustrated over seventy books for children. Born in Butte, Montana, he was an Army ski instructor in World War II. Kelly received his training at the Cornish School of Art in Seattle, Washington, and now divides his recreation time between tennis and gardening.